Max's Great Big World

Written by Rebecca Elkins

Artwork by Kelly Lincoln

ISBN 978-0-578-67201-4

Monday Creek Publishing LLC
mondaycreekpublishing.com

To Jeff, my rock. Thank you for supporting this dream every way you could. Your hard work and dedication to our family means everything.

To Adilyne and Jeffrey, my inspirations. Keep dreaming big, and wonderful things can happen. I love you both, even more than coffee.

Rebecca, aka Mommy

Thank you for being the Thelma to my Thelma and Louise.

Love, Kelly

Max loves the number five. He has been on this earth for five years now and on the fifth of June, he moved into his new house.

Max used to live in an apartment with his parents, but his dad's boss gave him something called a "transfer." Now Max has his very own bedroom and his very own backyard.

One day a neighbor lady came over with something wrapped in foil. A girl was standing behind her. Max introduced himself. "Hi, I'm Max, and I'm five." The girl was busy looking down at her tablet.

The girl's mom nudged her. The girl looked up long enough to say, "Hi, I'm Ellie," and then she looked back down at her tablet. Ellie's mom told Max that Ellie is eight. Max told Ellie how excited he was to have his very own backyard. Without even glancing up from her tablet, Ellie said, "Don't be excited. The backyard is boring." Then Ellie's mom gave Max the foil package that smelled like cookies and they walked away.

After he ate a cookie, Max walked over and stood by the sliding glass door that led to his backyard. Max's mom asked, "What's wrong, buddy?"

"Why do you think Ellie said the backyard is boring?" Max questioned.

His mom replied, "I don't know. Ellie seemed to be stuck in the world of her tablet. What do you see when you look into the backyard?"

Max saw a lot of things to explore. He said happily, "I see a great big world!"

Max's mom smiled. "Well, let's go outside and discover it!"

In the backyard, Max ran straight over to a dirt pile. He began to dig deep into the earth and uncovered gold nuggets.

He put them in a bucket and brought them to the bank.

Then he ran over to a tree stump and climbed it.

He became King of the Yard!

Later in the day, Max was enjoying a snack when he saw Ellie through the window of the house next door. Max waved happily at her, but it seemed like Ellie didn't notice. Max wondered why she looked so sad.

But Ellie did notice. How could Max be so happy? There was nothing out there to play with. She looked up at her babysitter.

Maybe she would play a game with her, but her babysitter was looking down at her phone, as always. Ellie already knew the answer, so she started scrolling through her tablet, looking for happiness.

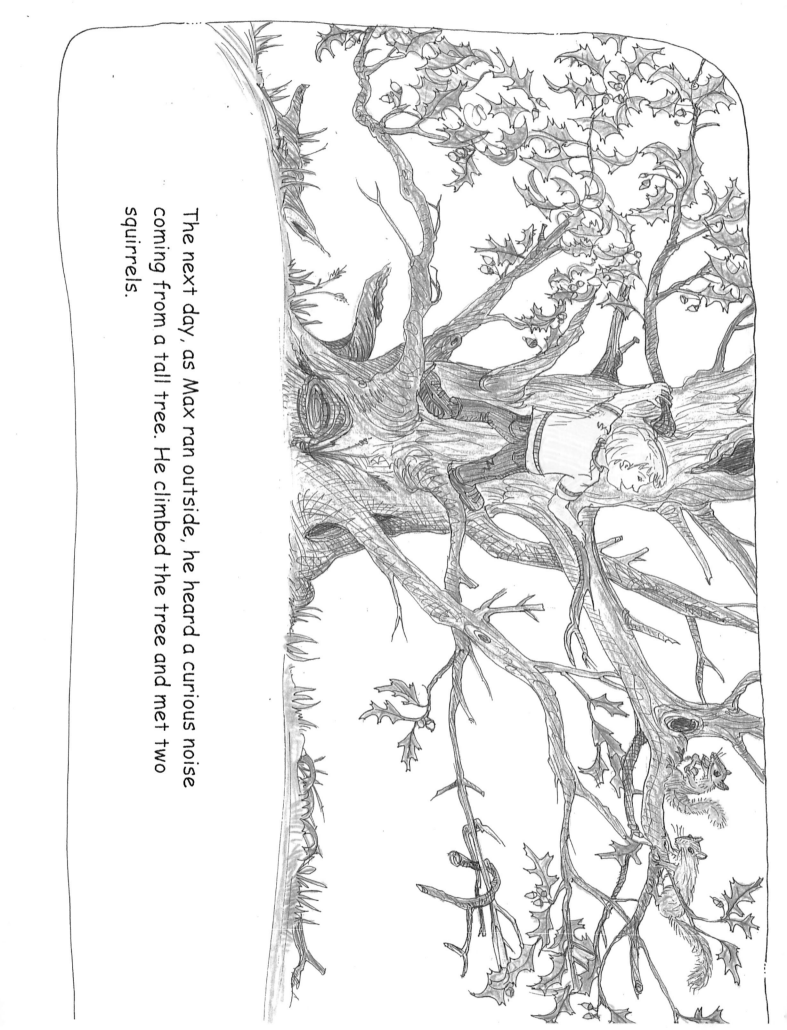

The next day, as Max ran outside, he heard a curious noise coming from a tall tree. He climbed the tree and met two squirrels.

The squirrels, Jim and Rootick, told Max all about the dog down the street who chases them to the corner of Max's house every day!

The squirrels always find a safe place in Max's backyard. Max loved listening to Jim and Rootick's stories.

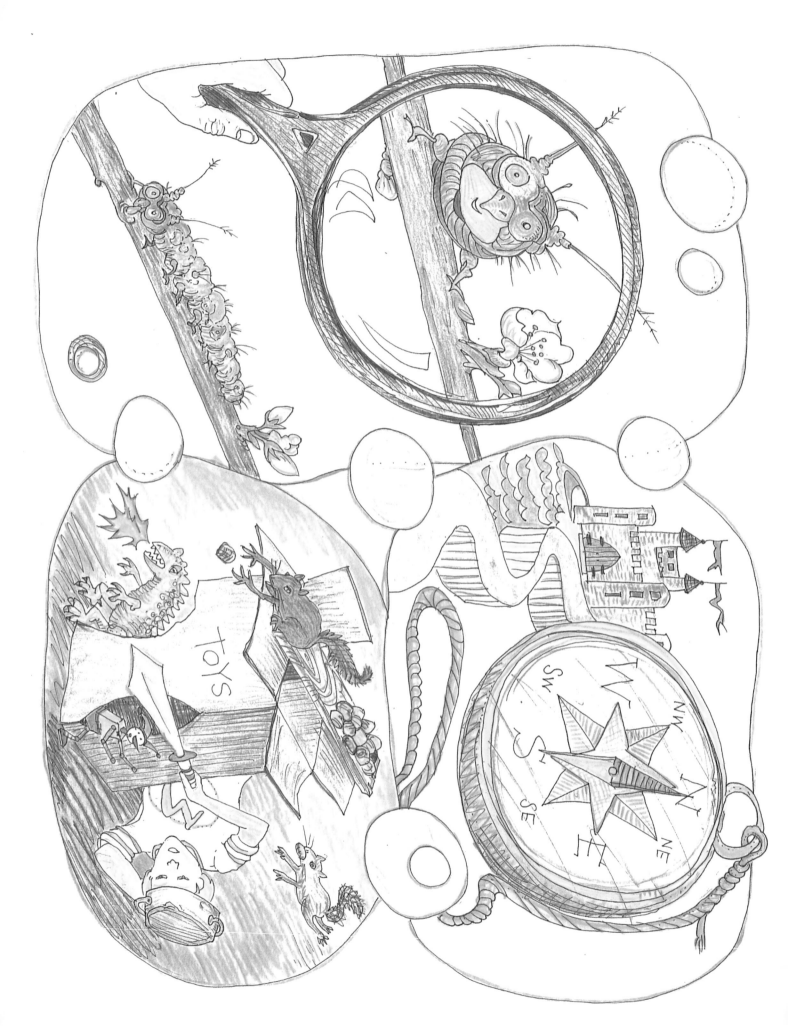

Day after day, Max played outside and had many amazing adventures.

Max would always wave for Ellie to come out and play. Ellie would just sit and watch from the window, then look back down at her tablet.

Finally, one day Ellie smiled at Max when he waved. Max asked his mom to take him next door to see if Ellie could come over. Max wanted to show Ellie how much fun the backyard could be!

As they headed into the backyard, Max ran over to his dirt pile.
Ellie hesitated, "Max, that's just dirt. What's so exciting about it?"
Max giggled, "We have to use our imaginations, Ellie!"

Ellie decided to play along. Perhaps giving her imagination a try would be fun.

Max's enthusiasm was contagious.

Soon they were exploring the moon with Jim and Rootick and making new friends.

Once they returned from the moon,

Max and Ellie became professional race car drivers.

After hours of adventures, Max and Ellie noticed it was getting dark outside. They collapsed in laughter.

"Ellie, why don't you ever play outside?" Max asked.

Ellie replied, "I don't know. I guess my tablet seemed easier, but today was so much fun! Thank you, Max."

"If you want," Max invited, "I can take you on all kinds of adventures!"

Ellie smiled at Max and as they looked up at the stars, Ellie began to see the great big world again.

ACKNOWLEDGMENTS

Thank you to my parents, Ron and Rose, for always pushing me to go for my dreams. No matter what, you both have been alongside me, supporting me.

Thank you to Carolyn Embree for giving your time to help me. *Max's Great Big World* would not be the story it is without your edits. Your kindness is inspiring.

Thank you to my beta readers. Your advice and encouragement were greatly appreciated.

Thank you to all our friends and family who continue to support us.

Lastly, thank you, readers, for picking *Max's Great Big World*, we hope you enjoy it!

About the Author

Rebecca Elkins, her husband Jeff and their two children, Adilyne and Jeffrey, call Ohio home. Rebecca enjoys spending time with her family, reading on her porch swing, and baking. As a teacher, Rebecca has read thousands of children's books. It has always been a dream of hers to write her own story. *Max's Great Big World* is her first, but definitely not her last. Rebecca hopes this story inspires readers to put down their electronics and open up their imaginations.

A little About the Illustrator

Kelly Lincoln graduated with honors from Pratt Institute of Art & Design, N.Y. She lives in a barn full of windows at Fernwood Farm & Studio, in Marietta, Ohio with many rescued mini-pigs & BIG playfull pigs, orphan sheep, cast-away chickens, lost & found dog & cat + one fine husband Mark Rila. Life is never dull. Please Remember: Art has No Rules! = Create Your Own Great Big World!

CPSIA information can be obtained
at www.ICGtesting.com
Printed in the USA
BVRC109912011121
620446BV00008B/263